Tabernacle Choir Aliens
by Rick Bennett

**The Adventures of Rich, Matt,
Laura, and Jonathan
(Supervised by Rick & Rita)**

INTRODUCTION

When we were little boys, my mom would make up bedtime stories for me and my brother Marsh. She titled them "Binky and Snooper" adventures. These are some of my fondest memories. This novella is my nod to those halcyon days, a bedtime story for my four children: Rich, Matt, Laura, and Jonathan. Merry Christmas about 50 years too late, as all are (or are about to be) grandparents themselves. So far, they've given Rita and me 19 grandchildren and (so far) 16 great-grandchildren. I had fun writing this. I hope you all have fun reading it.

Written by Rick Bennett. Edited by Marc Hunter, Brian Hailes, and Rita Bennett.

Cover artwork © 2024 by Rick Bennett, with Conference center photo EYN4RF by Norman Wharton, licensed from Alamy.com. Comic Book vector art licensed from 123RF.com.

Library of Congress Control Number: 9780970102690

Ebook (Kindle): 979-8-9909813-0-0

Paperback ISBN: 979-8-9909813-9-3

Hardback ISBN: 979-8-9909813-1-7

TABERNACLE CHOIR ALIENS

MAHUJAHPEDIAENTRY: In the year 18T5784 on Planet Earth, the Tabernacle Choir at Temple Square, formerly known as the Mormon Tabernacle Choir, provided the longest-running music broadcast in Earth's history. Widely regarded as

the epitome of the planet's choirs, tickets to the annual 24th of July celebration were increasingly hard to acquire. Security technology on this backward planet evolved to the point that stealthy visitations by extra-terrestrials was about to become impossible.

• • •

"Dad?" asked 14-year-old Laura, "We'll probably see some weird people on this TRAX train ride downtown."

"Maybe they'll think *we're* the weird ones," said Rick Henry to his daughter. "But it's worth the extra hour not to fight traffic. Tonight will be quite a treat."

"I like the idea of Heaven for the music," began her 16-year-old brother Matthew. That made his dad feel like he and his wife had made progress. But their son couldn't help but wipe the smile off his father's face. "But I'll prefer Hell with my friends."

Dad bit his lip, deciding not to start the evening with a fight that would last through the whole performance. He also followed his own father's advice: *Never miss an opportunity NOT to say something.* Instead, he looked out the left window of the train as it slowed and stopped at the Real Salt Lake soccer stadium.

A six-foot-tall lady with violet spiked hair boarded and took the seat facing the Henrys. Her knees almost touched Matthew's. She wouldn't have room to sit opposite the six-foot-five Rick. On the aisle beside her dad and despite herself, the petite blond Laura became an observer of both her father and of her older brother. She almost took out her iPhone to covertly record the unfolding game. This woman seemed to have a magnetic effect on both males.

Her brother's mouth hung open, his hormones duplicating a 4th of July fireworks finale in his brain. Her dad's matter-of-fact question to their new seatmate quite surprised Laura.

"Is your eye shade naturally violet?"

The woman smiled.

"They perfectly match your hair streak," continued Rick. "Just wondering if you are wearing contact lenses."

"I'm Alex," she said, extending her hand, looking first at Laura and then at the still-gaping Matthew. "Your children?"

"I'm Rick Henry." He shook her hand. "This is my daughter, Laura, and my son, Matthew. Two more are at home with their mom. My almost-18-year-old son, Rich, is leaving in October for a church mission to Alaska. And my youngest son, Jonathan, 12, is working on an Eagle Scout project tonight."

"These two both have blue eyes, and yours are green," she said as the train doors closed, and they resumed their trip to the Conference

Center in Salt Lake City. "I'll bet their mom has brown eyes."

"Yes," offered Laura. "Mom *does* have brown eyes."

"And the two brothers at home?" asked Alex, and it sounded to Laura as if this woman was really interested.

"Rich has hazel eyes, and Jonathan has brown eyes just like his mother," said Rick. "Back to *your* eyes?

"No, I'm not wearing contacts."

"Hum," muttered Rick. "Violet-colored eyes occur only due to albinism; but you do not display the other traits."

"Correct." Alex laughed unselfconsciously. "Most people don't know that fact. You're a doctor?"

"No, just a mathematician with a brain full of trivia. Ten miles wide and one inch deep."

"Dad's too self-depreciating." Laura playfully elbowed her dad. "He invented some electronics the government needed."

"A mathematician and electrical engineer wearing a superhero shirt this summer evening?" asked Alex.

"The kids gave me this shirt," said Rick, "which I've been looking for an excuse to wear. Oh, and a mathematician can design electronics simply by learning Ohm's Law."

"He's also a composer." Matthew finally broke out of his trance. "The 8-year-old children from our church are singing one of his songs tonight at the conference center. Accompanied by the Tabernacle Choir."

"Really?" Alex abruptly stood and rocked toward the aisle as the train slowed. "I wish I could find out more about your most interesting family. Unfortunately, I must get off at this stop to pick up my car. Pleased to meet you Laura, Matthew, and Rick."

After she departed and they started moving again, Matthew spoke first.

"She was babacious!"

"I'm surprised you didn't drool," said Laura.

"Hey!" began Matthew.

"Tell me what you observed," said Rick, quickly diffusing a sibling spat.

"Violet Mohawk with shaved sides," began Matthew. "Modest caftan. That was one hottie of mass destruction."

His sister rolled her eyes.

"Laura?" asked their dad.

"Uh, kind a mystery, those eyes. What do you think, Daddio?"

"Well, violet hair aside," Rick nodded. "Didn't notice any piercings or tattoos, but I sincerely doubt she associates with any of Mom's scripture-study group. Let's just say we met an interesting human being."

"She had it over those freaks that just got on," whispered Matthew as a co-ed group of gothic/face-painted/multi-pierced/tattooed teens skulked onboard.

One caught his attention and actually made eye contact with Matthew. Seven feet tall and red skin. As the man passed them to find a seat, Matthew noticed an honest-to-goodness tail trailing behind his full-length red robe. "Are those people actually from this planet?"

The ride into Salt Lake City proceeded in relative silence. The full moon and several departing passengers' costumes created an eerie out-of-this-world ambience that hung in Rick's mind. Several of the unusual riders commented on Rick's Hulk/Spiderman/Jedi shirt as they got off at the ballpark for a Bee's baseball game. The goths, along with the red-skinned giant sporting the tail, got off near some 9th-street condos. The cosplay Satan again made eye contact with Matthew.

"Dad, did you see that?"

"See what, Matt?" asked Rick.

"Never mind." An involuntary shiver went through his son.

The smell of second-hand cannabis hung with the Henry family as they continued the ride downtown. Rick and the kids exited the train and went to the Blue Lemon Restaurant for a quick dinner before they had to be seated in the conference center.

• • •

"You have the tickets?" asked Matthew.

"Yes, oh thou nervous one," answered his dad.

The three stood in line by the press entrance to the LDS Conference Center, waiting for the doors to open.

"I wonder why Scott gave us media-door tickets?" Laura looked up at her dad quizzically.

"He's the general manager of the choir," said Rick. "He always comes up with great tickets. These seats even have assigned numbers."

"At least our line is in the shade," said Laura. "That July sun would be giving us all skin cancer."

"These are only six rows back from the center stage," said Matthew as he looked over his dad's shoulder at the tickets. "I wonder if there'll be any girls nearby, or if we're going to be surrounded by church muckety-mucks?"

"Ah yes, girls." Rick suddenly got a mischievous look and turned toward the back of their line and yelled: "Hey, if you teenage girls think every swell boy on Earth is already taken, my son here doesn't have a girlfriend."

Matthew did a face plant. So did his sister. The chuckling line started to move, so Rick didn't have to deal with immediate fallout. He figured he'd have to wait.

Inside the conference center, they wound through the security line. Scott Barrack, their *connected* neighbor who provided tonight's tickets, greeted them.

"Rick, glad you got here early," said the choir general manager. "Hi Matt and Laura. Follow me and I'll show you to your seats."

Laura nudged her brother. "Wow, first class treatment."

Matthew, still in a snit about his dad's over-the-top statement outside, silently huffed alongside them. His tennis shoes squeaked along the marble floor. Scott led them down the center aisle and proudly pointed to the *RESERVED* placard on the aisle seat and removed the white ribbon blocking off the entire row.

"Rick, why don't you sit on the aisle? Your kids can sit next to you." At their raised eyebrows across the empty row, Scott added: "After your Primary class gets done singing, they can come down here and sit with you and their soon-to-arrive parents." Whereby Scott moved the reserved sign and ribbon three seats to their left.

"Wonderful!" exclaimed Rick. "Glad their folks can see this in person. Thank you, my friend."

Before Matthew could scoot in ahead of his sister, as he didn't want to sit next to his rude father, a toe-headed teenage girl came up to him from the front row and asked, "I heard your dad say you didn't have a girlfriend. My great-grandfather said it was okay if I maybe could sit by you? I'm Sheila Oaks and I have a bag of Twizzlers."

If the violet-haired/violet-eyed lady on TRAX had smitten him, this girl absolutely struck him dumb. Rick thought, *Sheila Oaks, great-granddaughter of Dallin H. Oaks, president of the Quorum of Twelve Apostles?* Wanting to rescue his son from possible brain damage, he said, "We'd be delighted to have you sit with us."

Matthew snapped out of his stupor and led the young lady into their row, having her sit between him and his sister. Laura looked like she wished her dad had commented on *her* availability in the waiting line. Their father looked down in the front row, where he caught the apostle smiling at him. He nodded back and took his own seat.

The program kicked off, and the guest celebrities got introduced to the audience. LDS opera soprano Rachel Willis-Sørensen joined movie star Neal McDonough on stage.

"Hey Dad," whispered Laura. "Isn't that guy the psycho albino in the Bruce Willis movie *Red 2*?"

"Now that you mention it," began her dad. And he thought, *What's with eyes all of a sudden?*

The evening had long passed surreal in the mind of Matthew, his heaven-sent date delighted in tormenting him by holding his hand. She offered him a twizzler with her other hand, which she put into his mouth. After he bit down, she proceeded to put the other end in her mouth and chomped toward him. To his credit, he tried to act nonchalant in maintaining the grip on her other hand and chewed toward those lips. Both were oblivious as parents of Rick and Rita's Primary class edged by them to take their reserved seats. Early on, when the opera diva sang the aria from *The Marriage of Figaro*, Rick figured his son was quite happy holding hands with Shelia Oaks and re-enacting the spaghetti scene from *Lady and the Tramp* cartoon. But Laura's comment about the albino character had Rick focusing on eyes. Even close to the stage, though, he couldn't really see eye colors. He wished he'd brought his opera glasses. He also wished the Oaks girl had shared some Twizzlers with him, as the unmistakable smell seemed to permeate the whole row, now filled with parents of his Sunday students.

These performances always featured organist Richard Elliot, who never ceased to wow the audiences with his one big solo number. That came at a rather unexpected time, as McDonough announced the special guests.

"We're proud to welcome the 8-year-old Primary class from the Eagle Crest 2nd Ward of the Church of Jesus Christ of Latter-day Saints singing a song composed by their teacher Rick Henry." The spotlight then shown right on his seat in row six. "Rick Henry, please come onstage and join your wife."

Gulp. *My wife! Here? What the...?* Audience applause jolted Rick to his feet and an usher guided him to stairs on the right. As he passed the orchestra pit on his left and ascended the stairs, his wife, Rita, along with the ex-psycho-albino movie star, met him onstage.

"Cool shirt," said McDonough.

His wife leaned forward with her mouth to his ear. "I *told* you that you might want to wear a suit tonight."

Since she'd been wired for sound, her admonishment broadcast to the entire 22,000-person audience. Which laughed and applauded. In on the appearance of their mother, Matthew and Laura clapped enthusiastically.

Rick would have said *No crap, darlin'!* but feared anything he said would be equally public.

"And joining the Tabernacle Choir on Temple Square," continued McDonough, "Please welcome Rick and Rita's eight-year-olds."

On cue, in marched their smiling students. The entire choir stood at that moment. Richard Elliot jumped off the theatre organ bench and ran to a harpsichord. He started vamping the first verse as McDonough announced: "Accompanied by the choir, the Henry's Eagle Crest 2nd Ward children will sing Rick's composition, *Jesus Needs All of our Voices*." With that, the choir started humming and conductor Mac Wilburg cued the kids to begin:

Jesus needs all of our voices,

Make every one sing loud and strong.

The high ones,

The low ones,

The glad ones, especially the sad ones,

Our choir making Earth ring with song.

The entire orchestra repeated the melody as Richard Elliot raced from the harpsichord to the piano and pounded the same melody, but in four octaves. At Wilburg's cue, the class sang the second verse, accompanied by the again-humming choir.

Jesus invites all of Earth's families,

To join in our heavenly song.

The sisters,

The brothers,

Don't forget all of the others,

Homes echoing praise loud and long.

Then, as the orchestra repeated the same melody, Richard Elliot raced from the piano to the organ, pulled out all the stops, and made the entire Conference Center echo with a full-throated sound like the Sistine Chapel pipe organ. Rick spotted conspiratory smiles and winks from two of his children, Moses Feil and Callie Hallstrom, before the third verse began. He prayed the two kids didn't do their usual sound effects. This time, the entire choir sang along. Because the children were all perfectly wired for sound, their voices carried above the adult singers behind them. *Oh no!* thought both Rick and Rita, who knew what Moses and Callie had in mind.

Jesus inspires all of creation,
Even rocks and trees will sing,
With mountains,
And canyons,
The *lamb* and the *lion* companions,
All sing to their Lord and their King.

The pipe organ played the same tune as previous verses, but it now sounded like a carnival calliope. Pictures of a merry-go-round appeared against the stage backdrop. Actual movies of animals on a carousel projected from conference center screens. *Not* to their surprise, Rick and Rita heard Callie call, "Baaa!" when they sang the word "lamb," and Moses roared accompanying the word "Lion." Organist Richard Elliot outright laughed and nearly lost concentration on the last musical phrase. Several Tabernacle Choir members also couldn't stifle snickers.

Standing beside their class, Rick shot the two delinquents a stern look. Rita just shook her head. Floating cameras caught everyone's reaction: the organist, the choir members, and even their two chagrinned teachers. Raucous audience applause drowned out the final lyrics. McDonough had trouble pulling himself together to move the program forward. He finally sputtered to Rick: "I don't think the suit would have helped. Spiderman, the

Hulk, and those other superheroes on your shirt clearly set the tone for your class."

Rick and Rita did a group hug as the children ran up to them, which evoked even more audience reaction. And then, uncharacteristically, organist Richard Elliot slid off the bench and joined the group. He took a microphone from one of the stagehands and raised his hands to calm auditorium.

"This was a great composition. I wanted to thank you and share the news that your song will appear in the new children's song book."

Rick couldn't hear anything else above the enthusiastic resumption of cheers and applause. He didn't register the noise, because of Elliot's Violet eyes. Violet, just like the lady on the train. *What in the Sam Hell?* he thought. Then, almost dizzy, he glanced at the applauding choir members. He spotted half a dozen violet eyes in both men and women. And not an albino in the bunch. *What in the Sam Hell indeed!*

Finally, at the invitation of McDonough, the children and their teachers were invited to sit with the Henry children—all four of them, now—in row six. Laura, Matthew and Sheila Oaks were joined by Rick's sons Rich and Jonathan. The remainder of row six now comprised all sixteen parents of their Primary Class, who anxiously awaited their now-superstar children.

This is the best-kept secret in the universe, thought Rick. *Literally. How did they put this all together without my figuring it out*? But more importantly, *where did all these violet-eyed people come from? What gene pool? Dare I ask, what planet?*

As they filed down the stairs to row six, Richard Elliot hurried back to the organ and performed a spectacular improvisation on the theme *Jesus Needs All of our Voices*. The entire conference center rocked with enthusiasm. And in testament to solid construction, the balconies didn't come crashing down.

"Rick," Rita leaned close to her husband as they sat through the rest of the program, "We have a limousine waiting to take our family home, so you don't need to stand in those massive TRAX lines."

Of course! thought Rick. *This modern-day top-secret adventure stood right up there with D-Day's Operation Overlord. I should have put two and two together, given that this* was *our Sunday class performing. Must have been my focus on deploying the CIA/NSA project that erased all situational awareness.*

Rick couldn't honestly remember anything about the rest of the program. His brain had been well and truly short-circuited. And he didn't expect the attention on row six when all the dancers, performers, and the guest stars took their encore bows. Rita elbowed him to stand with their entire group in multiple spotlights, simultaneous with a pipe organ reprise of their musical number. At long last, after the audience stood while the Church leadership left their front-row seats and Sheila Oaks rejoined her family, choir general manager, Scott Barrick, appeared and guided their elated conga line to an underground staging area where everyone got rides in their respective limousines. Nine chauffeured cars, one for each family. And even after a most eventful evening, Rick's surprises hadn't ended. At the head of the nine black Lincolns, none other than the spiked violet-hair lady, with whom they'd talked on the train ride into Salt Lake City, held the car door for them. After which she strutted around to the driver's side and assumed her seat behind the wheel.

No sooner had the family gotten into the car than Laura piped up: "I think they liked your song, Dad."

"Richard Elliot sure did a spectacular performance on the organ!" effused Rita, who tried to prod Rick into a celebratory mood.

"And it's going to be in the new children's song book!" said their eldest son, Rich. "I can't wait to get on my mission in Alaska and show people Dad's name."

Even this didn't evoke any reaction from their father.

"Dad!" exclaimed Matthew, wistfully wiping red from this corner of his mouth, "Did you see who's driving us?"

Sensing they needed an explanation, their driver interrupted.

"I picked up my limo when I got off TRAX, and then drove up the mountain to chauffeur Rita and your other two sons to the conference center," said Alex.

Rick just shook his head.

Alex continued: "I found out on the ride downtown that you guys trained with the Canadian National Ski Team in June on the Whistler Mountain glacier. Do you remember people on the Snowbird chairlifts yelling 'Moose, Moose, Moose' at you as you skied below us?"

"Yeah," said Laura. "Jonathan wore his moose hat as he showed off."

"That was a few of us from the choir," said Alex. "No wonder you looked so good. You trained with the world freestyle champion."

"Well, the retired world champion," said Matthew. "Wayne Wong still taught a great class."

Their mom jumped in. "These guys love to show off jumps and flips."

"Matt, Rich!" scolded Laura. "Put your eyes back into their sockets."

"What about me?" asked Jonathan.

"You're pre-teen," snickered Laura. "You haven't been whacked with the hormone stick yet."

"You guys are being rude," said their mother. "Don't embarrass Alex. We had a very nice ride downtown."

From the front seat, their driver interrupted. "Rita, as I told you on the ride from your home, I rode TRAX with your husband for two stops. We had a conversation about eye color, and something tells me he made some observations about certain choir member's eyes."

"Rick?" asked Rita.

"I just connected some dots," said Rick, breaking out of his stupor. "Some violet dots, eh Alex?"

"And?" the driver asked.

Rick finally loosened up. "My song, *Jesus Needs All of our Voices,* should include a fourth verse about the ones from off-planet, too."

"What!" exclaimed Laura a split second before the same exclamation erupted from her three brothers.

"I'm just fooling with you guys," said Rick. To himself, he thought: *Alex's silence indicates I hit the nail on the head. I think we'd better have a chat after she drops the family off.* "Kids, I'm just in a science fiction mood, tonight. Don't pay my ramblings any attention."

Rita's raised eyebrows, facing him in the limo, screamed the word "*Nah!*" Okay, they'd been married twenty years, and she could see right through him.

Jonathan started playing with the AM/FM radio in their compartment and ironically tuned into a late-night talk show on Unidentified Anomalous Phenomena, or UAPs, formerly popularized as UFOs. George Noory interviewed a guest on his *Coast to Coast AM* program.

"Now Pete, you say you were kidnapped by aliens and taken aboard a UAP?"

"Yessir, I was. And they done some...er...sexual experiments on me."

Laughter from Alex, their driver, interrupted the program. "I remember abducting Pete in our flying saucer."

The kids all shot Rick a startled look. Even Rita snapped to attention.

"Yeah," continued Alex. "Took him into our spaceship, loved him up, and then turned him into a horny toad."

"Dad!" screamed Laura. But Rich and Matthew started laughing, which drew even more shocked looks from their sister. "Jonathan joined the hilarity and slugged his sister in the arm."

Rick leaned over and turned off the radio. "Our driver quoted a line from the movie *O Brother, Where Art Thou?* Loosen up, Bug."

Laura opened the sunroof. "I need some fresh air in the full moon. Smells like twizzlers in here."

Whereupon she stood on the seat and let the July night wind blow her hair. Jonathan stood up beside her, and they had an unintelligible conversation, punctuated by snickering. Down below, Rick spoke loudly enough to be heard above the whistling wind from above: "Rita, shall we invite Alex to come in and have some midnight cheesecake with us?"

"By all means," answered Rita. "Alex, are you available for some late dessert?"

"Thank you. I could use some calories."

Rick spent the rest of the ride putting together some questions for their driver. Rita sat back and savored the new-car/twizzler-tinted smell of the limo. The kids all squeezed into the sunroof opening and let the still-ninety-degree wind blast through their hair.

• • •

"Mrs. Henry, this cheesecake is out of this world," said Alex.

"Out of this world," Laura snickered. "Just couldn't help yourself?"

They all sat around the kitchen island; the two oldest boys focused on capturing at least one caramelized cherry with each bite. The youngest, Jonathan, seemed awed by their tall guest's violet hair and matching eyes. Rita busied herself serving everyone, while their dad joined Jonathan in his fascination with the charming driver.

Rick decided to have a private conversation with Alex and clapped his hands twice. "Chop-chop guys. It's after midnight, and we have church tomorrow."

"Rich, Matt, we have a guest!" scolded their mom. "You licked your plates. Rich, promise me you won't do that on your mission."

"Even for Eskimos in Alaska?" Rich quickly put his now-clean plate down and made for his bedroom before she could vaporize him with her stare.

"G'nite, Alex," said Matthew as he grabbed Laura's arm to head for their rooms. Then pausing, he asked, "By the way, Alex, did you see a guy about a head taller than you, with red skin and a tail? And I could swear I saw him following our car tonight when us kids had out heads out the sunroof."

"Matthew, bed!" scolded Rita. Alex seemed taken aback by Matt's question. Rick made a note to delve further.

Jonathan had barely started his dessert, having been intent on their guest, and quickly dug into his own cheesecake. Rita ignored him and hurried, rinsing the dishes and loading the dishwasher.

"Dear, can I borrow Alex for a second?" asked Rick. "I'd like to show her my library."

"Okay," said Rita. "Just don't bore her with your sci-fi conspiracy theories."

"Thank you, Rita, for a wonderful dessert," said Alex as she followed Rick down the hall to his study. Then to Rick: "Tell me about these *theories.*"

Rick winked as he gestured toward a wingback leather chair next to a floor-to-ceiling bookcase and across from his own swivel chair in front of multiple computer screens and his 3D printer. As she sat, Alexa motioned to books within her reach.

"Rita wasn't joking," she said. "Herbert, Pournelle, Niven, Anthony, Silverberg, Ringo, Hubbard. And these are just the guys near me on the shelf."

"That's nothing compared to some religious texts I have in the basement." Rick tilted his head sideways, waiting for a reaction. Alex didn't disappoint.

"You must be talking about Hyrum Andrus and Hugh Nibley?"

"You really cut to the chase," said Rick. "The late Hugh Nibley opined that on all inhabited worlds, there may be many different and exotic plants and animals, but mankind will always be the same. And the late BYU scholar Hyrum Andrus was threatened with excommunication for preaching that, during the Millennium, we will be a space-faring race, taking the ordinances of salvation to all of God's creations."

"Both were right."

"Okay, Alex," Rick leaned back in his leather recliner. "Tell me your story."

"Two words. Mahijah and Mahujah."

"Ah ha! Hugh Nibley's 1977 commentary on the story of Enoch, whose city was taken from the earth prior to the flood."

"And?" asked Alex, scooting forward on her chair.

"Nibley said that the names, Mahijah, from the city Mahujah, were not available when quoting Enoch by the prophet in *The Pearl of Great Price*. They were only unearthed in the *Dead Sea Scrolls* and not translated until the mid-1970s. You people, whoever you are and wherever you're from, knew these names and figured we were somehow kindred spirits."

"And?" Alex asked again.

"And why me? Why now?"

"Because prophecies told us to expect that you would be the one to save our mission back to Earth."

Rick swallowed and, with wide eyes and raised eyebrows, just stared at his alien guest. She didn't say a word. His eyes got wider as the violet hair vanished, morphing into blond curls. And her eye color changed to bright green, matching his.

"Your daughter told Matthew to put his eyes back in his head," said Alex. "That's good advice for you, huh?"

"I'll say," gasped Rick. "You have complete control over your DNA. Hair color, eye color. My questions are cascading into an avalanche."

"Start asking," said the now-green-eyed blonde.

"Maybe you could start by morphing back into our violet-haired/violet-eyed driver. If any of the kids stick their heads in here, we don't want every teenager on the mountain to know we have a real, honest-to-gosh ET visiting."

"To do that, I urgently need to metabolize some carbs. Might I have a couple more pieces of cheesecake and a big glass of milk?"

"Done," said Rick as he went to the kitchen and returned with cake and milk.

Alex attacked the food like a refugee after an arduous border crossing. A literal trek across a parsec-sized border. Then, her instantaneous transformation drew another gasp from Rick.

"Why are you people in the Tabernacle Choir?" He paused. "I mean, why not the Coro Polifonico in Italy? Or the Kammerchor in Berlin?"

"Or maybe you think we'd join the Sistine Chapel Choir, constituted as the Pope's personal choir?"

"That's also a possibility."

"I'll quote the prophecy that brought us here: *And your journey shall be saved by the man who pens the New Song ending with 'rocks and trees will sing, with mountains, and canyons, with lamb and lion companions, all sing to her Lord and her king.'*"

"Not so fast, Hoss!" Rick slapped his knee. "I just wrote those words this year. Oh, and that organist, Richard Elliot, is one of you. Right?

"Yes."

"Okay, he's been with the choir over 30 years. How did you decide on the Tabernacle Choir and Utah three decades ago?"

"Simple. That prophecy was written by a fellow named Mahijah. Ring a bell?"

"Like I said, the book of *Moses* in the *Pearl of Great Price*."

"Correct. We got here nearly 40 years ago and have been waiting for *The New Song*." Alex leaned forward, resting her elbows on her knees. "We've been waiting for you. What better place to hide in plain sight than with the Tabernacle Choir? After all, you're the only people on the planet whose religious texts identified the two names."

"If that prophecy were written by Mahijah, it couldn't have been written in the English language! It had to be translated from...what...the original, pure, pre-flood language."

"I see you know your Bible," she said. "Yes, but you'll have to agree our translation was flawless."

"Unbelievable!" Rick stared at his guest for what seemed over a minute. "But..."

"But what?" Alex made both eyes alternate between green and violet, clearly toying with him.

"But I'm supposed to...? Cut out that distracting eye thing! I'm supposed to save your journey?"

"In a nutshell, yup."

"Just thinking, though, isn't Richard Elliott is a native of Baltimore, Maryland?" Rick snapped his fingers. "That's in close proximity to Washington, D.C."

"He is our leader," said Alex. "We set up foolproof identities for our team based near the nation's capital."

"Nothing's fool proof. You may have been able to steal birth certificates from dead babies and reposition yourselves back in the 1970s, but the NSA and the CIA are using today's computer spidering technology to nab foreign agents and felons on the lam who used dead-baby tricks to generate identities."

"We're nab-proof. Richard was here long enough to build real backgrounds from scratch. Fake births, fake bank and school records, report cards, social security numbers, income tax payments for over 40 years. Just waiting for the rest of his crew to land and assume those identities."

"Wait, that would put you in your 70s," gasped Rick. "You can't be over 30!"

"I'm way older than that, which we'll get to later."

"But you join the Tabernacle Choir. Waiting in plain sight." Rick sighed. "I'm impressed. You're playing the long game, no pun intended."

"We *thought* this was fool proof, but—"

"But not damn-fool proof," Rick interrupted.

"Your little instant-DNA-sequencing project for Homeland Security can spot us a mile away."

"Oops!" Rick reached behind his credenza and emerged with a device no larger than a cellphone. "Mind if I take a peek at your DNA?"

"I thought you'd never ask," came a sultry voice.

Rick immediately blushed but aimed the device toward her.

"Wow!" His blush disappeared immediately at a beep and blinking red screen on the scanner. "According to this, you're immortal?"

"Like I said, I'm way older than 70. But please explain."

"It's not just that specific markers or mutations associated with longevity are solid, but your stem cells have not mutated in the rest of your body. Like in regular, aging bodies. My scanner has concluded your cells do not age normally. They don't age at all! In other words—"

She interrupted: "In other words, your device flagged me immediately."

Rick scratched his chin. "You know, I just put this alarm in to flag immortal dudes who happen to be wandering amongst we of limited lifespans. A pet theory of mine."

"Like certain biblical characters who were blessed with immortality? Alex stood and perused his bookshelf. "Your wild-hare idea could spell doom for our mission to your planet."

"The best-laid plans often have S-N-A-PH-Us with a capital '*PH*.'"

"What's with the '*PH*?'"

"'*P*' for prophecy and '*PH*' rhymes with '*F*' if you know what I mean."

"Rick, the prophecy says you're supposed to save our mission to Earth," said the exasperated alien. "So far, I don't see the plus side. Only disaster."

"I don't get it. How is my device jeopardizing whatever brought you here?"

"You're recently delivered thousands of these devices to Homeland Security. They're about to be installed in all TSA airport passenger scanners. The choir—"

"I see," Rick interrupted. "The choir can't fly around the world without setting off alarms."

"And we've got a few more years before our mission can be completed," said Alex.

"What's the mission?" Rick paused. "Taking over the planet?"

"Hardly! We'll simply be announcing ourselves," she said. "But we haven't yet been given the go ahead. But a premature announcement of our presence here will cause irreparable harm. That's also in the prophecy."

"Okay. What do you want me to do?"

"We need you to take this functionality *out* of your DNA scanners."

"Big problem, Alex." Rick scratched the stubble on his chin. "Those devices have been shipped."

"But can't you do a remote firmware upgrade?"

"Nope. For security reason, I made sure that each unit was air gapped. No external connections of any kind are permitted. Too many bad actors around the world would hack into any connected devices."

"Oh," came out as more of a sigh.

"My neighbor across the street was a chief weapons officer on a nuclear submarine. We considered firmware changes using the same top-secret defense technology they use to update nuclear missile codes on the sub fleet, but air gapping won out as far less complicated. Any upgrades to the scanners must be sent as physical ROM chips."

"Rick, in less than two weeks, the choir is starting a world tour, with a first stop in Vatican City for a combined performance with the Sistine Chapel Choir."

"Whoa. And you guys can't get on an airplane without setting off alarms." Rick paused to consider his next question. "How many of you are in the choir?"

"Including our organist, 26."

"And you can't stay home?"

"Richard Elliott and two soloists are critical to the planned performance."

"I guess it's too late to bag the choir?"

"That's another part of the prophecy," Alex shrugged. "We don't exactly know why. We just...well...showed up for auditions. Had to jump through some ecclesiastical hoops, I might add."

"Oooookay. In two weeks, is it safe to say things are going straight to Hell?"

"According to our prophet Mahijah, the devil still thinks he can destroy all of God's creations. He must merely cause just one of the Creator's prophecies to fail, and he makes God into a liar, which will destroy *everything*."

"I noticed your reaction to Matthew's query about a red-skinned guy with a tail."

"Doesn't ring a bell."

He could tell something rang a bell alright. *You shouldn't ever play poker*, he thought. Her tells were mile wide. Rick decided *not* to press further and focused on the immediate issue.

"So, you're telling me that the fate of the world is in my hands?"

"No." Alex hung her head before looking him straight in the eye. "I'm telling you the fate of God Himself, and all of His creations, is in your hands."

"That is, if your prophet wasn't full of crap."

"He had the words of your song a few thousand years ago. Are you willing to take a chance?"

"Nuts!"

• • •

Rick Henry didn't sleep well that night. Or for very long. At 3:00 AM, his AI-driven defense system activated. Emergency back-up power came on, which meant something, or someone, had cut electricity to their house. Several simultaneous events combined to create pandemonium.

First, every light in the house came on, and bright spotlights turned the outside into daylight.

Second, even before battering rams of the invaders could position to break into both front and back doors, loudspeakers blared: "Alert, the police have been called. This home is protected by defensive tasers. Any attempt to breach the doors will activate those measures. You should have noticed signs front and back indicating intruders will be immobilized by AI-activated systems."

Finally, a message broadcast in Rick's voice: "If this is a home invasion, you're inviting a world of hurt. If not a criminal act, for your own protection, go before the police get here. We are watching on a closed-circuit monitor. Please step off the front porch and holster any weapons."

That last message barely completed before the front *and* back doors took their first hits. Being solid steel with multiple titanium deadbolts securing them, the rams barely made a dent. And the men wielding those devices didn't have enough time to make a second attempt, as tasers erupted in a 360-degree attack vector. Even though the attackers wore bullet-proof vests and helmets, at least one electrified barb connected with skin on each man. Whether on their bare necks from the pillars behind them, or through the unprotected sleeves of their arms, Rick saw a dozen men in tactical gear immobilized and twitching on the ground. The fact that their invaders had been neutralized put a plus in the good-news column.

In the big, fat minus column? All the flak jackets had the words '*POLICE*' stenciled across the back in big, white letters.

"Rita, someone has swatted us," said Rick.

Still groggy from too little sleep, she asked, "What's a swatting?"

"Darlin', that's when someone calls 9-1-1 and reports a serious criminal situation is underway to trick the police into sending a SWAT team to a high-risk situation." Rick paused and then said, "Hand me the microphone on your side of the bed. I need to diffuse this before they start shooting."

She quickly grabbed the mic and passed it to him.

Rick pushed the speak button, which overrode the AI warning broadcast. "This is Rick Henry, the homeowner. My wife and four children are safe, and there is no emergency. We've been swatted. So put your weapons on safety, and I'll be coming out the front door. Unarmed."

The picture-in-picture on their 80-inch flatscreen TV showed black-clad men dragging their recently tased companions off both the front and back porches.

"Kids, go to the safe room with your mother. Now!" They complied before Rick stepped out the front door with both hands raised.

A spotlight nearly blinded him, and a bullhorn voice said, "Put your hands behind your head and step off the porch."

Rick didn't argue, figuring one furtive move could get him turned into swiss cheese. The next thing he knew, two officers in SWAT gear bodily wrestled him to the ground and cuffed his hands behind him.

"You're under arrest!" said their obvious leader.

"What's the charge, officer?"

"Resisting arrest and physically assaulting law officers." They dragged him to his feet.

"You didn't announce that you were police," said Rick.

"We most certainly did."

"Au contraire my little cabbage head," said Rick. "I have high-resolution digital recording of your entire operation, complete with sound. So, unless you had a legitimate no-knock warrant, I suggest you stand down and uncuff me."

"Three of my men are injured, and a fourth is getting CPR from a likely heart attack. Tag, you're it, moron!"

"Your badge says Division Commander Berdon Styles," said Rick. "Computer, please send this entire dialogue, along with the complete video, to my attorney, Denver Snuffer, and to every major news station. Now."

"Cut the power!" screamed Commander Styles as he keyed his shoulder-mounted radio.

"We cut the power before we approached the porch," came the reply. "This guy's on some kind of backup."

Commander Styles stood speechless, his face turning beet red. Just then, from the loudspeaker above the front door: "This is now streaming to all the major television networks as well as to the Henry's attorney. Backup copies are secured in an encrypted AWS cloud account."

"Take this man downtown and secure the other occupants in the house," said the SWAT commander.

"You might not want to do that," said Rick.

The SWAT team seemed hesitant to obey the order. Styles repeated it. They should have disobeyed.

• • •

The team all wore full body armor, combat helmets with full face masks, and steel-reinforced gloves. Too bad they didn't have either air filtration masks or oxygen bottles. The entire house instantly filled with teargas, spiked with Mace. The team stumbled back out of the house, gagging and retching. The steel front door through which Rick had exited and the SWAT team had entered, *and* subsequently fled, slammed shut. Heavy duty exhaust fans inside the Henry home quickly expelled the offending mixture to the front and back yards through vents buried in the lawn.

Only Rick knew what to expect, and he'd been busy using a key he'd palmed before opening his front door to unlock his cuffs. Holding his breath and using now-free hands during the coughing confusion of his captors, he retrieved a specially designed mask and air filter he'd secreted in his pajama waistband and pulled it over his head. He then calmly walked toward the SWAT commander, affixed the handcuffs to wrists that conveniently protected the face of the now-prostrate man, and sat down beside him. A north wind quickly cleared the area, and it took about six minutes for the disabled men to cough and pass around bottled water with which they sloshed in their eyes. Commander Styles took a little longer, given the limitations imposed by his cuffs.

Sitting beside Styles, Rick's fluffy slippers rested next to the commander's size 13 combat boots. He took a bottle of water and rinsed the man's eyes.

"I told you sending those men into my house was a bad idea," said Rick.

The still-cuffed commander looked at the masked man seated next to him with real surprise. Rick removed his facemask, tucked it into his pajama waistband, and smiled at Styles, who jerked his right hand toward his sidearm only to discover the cuffs.

"You've knowingly assaulted a police SWAT group," spat Styles, still teary eyed from the toxic dose. "You're going to jail for a long time."

"Settle down, Hoss," said Rick. "I expect the television crews are going to show up momentarily, and I want to save you some embarrassment."

The SWAT commander blinked several times and managed to stifle further aggression. Rick continued.

"Now, would you mind telling my why you guys launched a no-knock raid on my home?"

Styles answered as calmly as he could: "We received a call from a woman at your listed number. She said a home invasion was in process and her family needed help. Shots were fired before the call abruptly disconnected."

"Sir, that call was a swatting." Rick then raised his voice. "Computer! Please unlock the safe room and send my family out the front door."

"Acknowledged," came the disembodied voice over the loudspeakers.

"Commander, please have your team stand down. I don't want my family shot."

"Lower your weapons, the family is coming out!" shouted Styles. Then, growling softly to Rick: "Get these damn cuffs off me before the news people show up."

Rick used his master handcuff key to free him as the Henry family—Rita, Rich, Matt, Laura and Jonathan—came out the front door. He then stood and raced to do a group hug with his wife and children. The tight-jawed commander followed.

"Might my men clear the house without further surprises?" asked Styles.

"Computer, deactivate defenses and let these men make sure no one else is hiding inside."

"Acknowledged," came the reply.

The edgy SWAT team looked to Styles, who nodded toward the door. Five men carefully stepped over the now inert taser wires strewn across the porch. Ten minutes later, they exited at the same time two news vans arrived, one from the ABC affiliate and one from NBC.

"Decision time," said Rick as he rejoined Commander Styles.

"Sir," said a tall policeman, obviously a close aide to the commander. "We really didn't announce ourselves. I recommend you cut our losses and turn this into a tactical win."

The commander reluctantly agreed with his subordinate's advice and whispered, "I'd be grateful if you help me do damage control for our mistakes, tonight."

Rick held out both hands, an invitation to be handcuffed on camera, but Styles motioned to the contrary. The Channel 4 and 5 crews did their sound checks while portable lights focused on the man with the most stripes on his sleeve. The short interview confirmed that the Henry home had indeed been *swatted* and that none of the occupants had been injured.

"Law enforcement will do all we can to apprehend the 9-1-1 caller who falsely reported a hostage situation at this address," concluded SWAT Commander Styles.

Asked for his reaction, Rick responded: "This could have ended far differently, and I'm glad my family is safe."

• • •

Later that morning at church, the bishop asked Rick to speak briefly during the meeting and share their adventures, both at the conference center and later with the bogus 9-1-1 call. Every member of the Henry family got peppered with questions in hallways after the meetings had concluded. At home, they didn't answer either the door or their cellphones. Most of their neighbors realized they needed privacy. A few more of the socially oblivious quickly figured it out when nobody responded to a knock on the door or when their phone calls went to voicemail.

Sunday became Monday, and Rick did answer a call when an interesting caller ID appeared got his attention: the Tabernacle Choir Organist himself.

"Rick Henry here."

"Hi. It's Richard Elliot calling. May I drop by, today?"

"Any time it's convenient for you," said Rick. "Just text this number when you're out front, and I'll be sure to answer the door."

An hour later, tabernacle organist, Richard Elliot, sat in Rick's den.

"I noticed your grand piano in the living room, and your keyboard here," said Elliot. "Is this where you composed your children's song?"

"Yeah, I use Garage Band to lay down the tracks and experiment with different orchestrations."

"I bet you play the organ in church meetings."

"No," laughed Rick. "I'm dyslexic and don't easily sight-read music. Thank Heaven for Garage Band and spell-checking computers. Otherwise, I'd be robbing liquor stores for a living."

Elliot crossed legs, one red and one blue tennis shoe sticking out from his jeans. "A few of us in the choir may devolve into that profession, knocking over liquor stores, if we can't ever get on an airplane again."

"Off the subject, but is your choice of shoe color symbolic of your complete DNA acrobatics?"

"Oh that," Elliot chuckled. "Some of us went to BYU and some to the University of Utah. The blue and the red. This is just a nod to both schools. As for the eye color and what you call DNA acrobatics, I think we're doomed."

"Your chances of making it through airport security?" opined Rick. "You are well and truly screwed. It's my fault completely, and I am profoundly sorry."

"You can't figure out a way to change that functionality in your device?"

"Right now, what I'm trying to figure out is who faked the 9-1-1 call that jeopardized my family," said Rick. "And are we still in some kind of danger?"

As if on cue, a rather large drone appeared to be peeking through the plum tree in front of Rick's den window. A drone that had weapons mounted on a platform below four heavy duty rotors. Seconds before automatic weapons obliterated the plum tree and shattered the picture window, Rick jumped forward and swept Richard Elliot out of his leather chair onto the floor.

"Computer, call that SWAT commander's personal cellphone and get us help!" yelled Rick amid the staccato fire and exploding glass.

"Acknowledged," came the reply.

But even before the gunfire ceased, Rick's eldest son, Rich, rushed from the garage with a baseball bat and smashed two of the four rotors on the drone in a single swing. Amidst the smell of gunpowder and ozone from short-circuited electric motors, the machine dropped to the ground. Rich kept whacking it until not only all four rotors ceased to function, but the cellphone-controller pod was obliterated. And just to be sure all electronics were kaput, Matthew followed him from the garage pulling a hose, and sprayed down the smoking remains.

"Dad, we got it!" yelled Rich.

Rick burst out the front door, looking aghast at his bat-wielding/hose-spraying sons.

"You guys could have been killed!" he yelled.

"Well duh!" mocked Rich as the mist from Matt's spray formed a cloud around fallen tree branches and the drone wreckage.

"Hey, can we keep the machine guns?" added Matthew.

"Jeeze Louise!" scolded Rick. "Not only *no. Hell no!*."

Jonathan and Laura Henry got into the photo action as well. Laura held a yardstick at several angles while Jonathan shot photos on his Android cellphone.

"Jon, Bug," said Rick, calling Laura by his pet name for her. "What are you doing? That could still be dangerous."

"Not now, Dad," said Jonathan. "I'm going to check the Web and find out who made this bad boy."

By then, it looked to Rick like the whole neighborhood had gathered on the street to see the source of the racket.

"Sir," said Rick back inside the house to his tabernacle organist/alien guest. "This is about to become Grand Central Station combined with the NSA mitigation team. I don't know what's going to happen or how long it will take. You don't want to be here when the balloon goes up."

"Agreed," said Elliot. "Do you have any idea how we're going to solve our setting off TSA airport alarms?"

'Here, take this." Rick's shoes crunched across broken glass as he went to his desk and retrieved the DNA scanner. "I don't know what's going to happen around here. Maybe you guys can figure out a way around this."

"Long shot?"

"Better than no shot. Now, get outta Dodge."

"Adios, amigo," said the departing Richard Elliot.

• • •

Several neighbors soon joined them. And less than five minutes later, a dark Suburban and two NSA...*Men in Black*...arrived.

"Son, I am confiscating that cellphone," said the MIB riding shotgun. Jonathan still busied himself taking photos of the downed drone.

"Jon!" yelled Rick to his son. "Do *not* give that man your phone. Go into the house immediately!"

"Stop!" responded the NSA agent.

Jonathan didn't need to decide which order to obey. He ran into the house.

"Let me see some identification," commanded Rick.

"Your home is now under the protection of the National Security Agency," said the agent as he handed Rick his identification. "We are *not* leaving without that young man's cellphone."

"Agent Dan Boyce," said Rick as he scanned the ID and then snapped a picture of it with his own cellphone. "Did your parents toilet train you at gunpoint?"

"Give me that!" Agent Boyce lunged for the phone, but Rick quickly slid it into his front jeans pocket.

"Lay one hand on me and you will leave here in a body bag."

The driver had joined his fellow MIB in time to overhear the threat.

"What did you say?" asked Boyce.

"Computer!" said Rick without turning toward the house. "Target these two men with head shots. Execute them both if either one makes physical contact with me."

"Acknowledged," sounded from the porch speaker.

Aghast, both NSA men stepped backward, away from Rick. About twenty neighbors also increased their distance from the Henry home.

"I wonder what our billionaire next door is going to do next," said Regan Tingey, an immediate neighbor. Rick Henry's financial status had been shared with a few close friends. The instantaneous DNA sequencer had been a game changer, and Wall Street rewarded him appropriately.

"Probably replace his windows with bullet-proof glass," said John Walsh, who walked up from down the block. "He can afford it."

The two NSA MIBs quickly loaded the destroyed drone into the back of their Suburban before anybody else could take pictures of the formerly deadly device.

"Good idea, bullet-proof windows," said Rick to ex-Navy captain Walsh. "I'm going to take care of that right now."

With that, Rick disappeared through his front door

"Kids, front and center!" called their dad. "The four quickly joined he and Rita in the living room. "Rich, how did you and Matthew get out there so fast with the baseball bat and the hose?"

Two boys turned toward their youngest brother, who nervously rocked from foot to foot. Rick raised his eyebrows and waited for the twelve-year-old to fess up.

"Last night after you brought Alex more food, I snuck a look into your den and saw her hair change from blond to violet." Jonathan paused. "Then I knew you weren't joking in the car last night and that she really is an extraterrestrial. So—"

Rich interrupted his brother. "So...we held a kids council and decided to prepare for, as gonzo Hunter S. Thompson describes it, the inevitable shit rain."

"Rich!" scolded his mother. "Language."

"And?" Rick waited for more explanation.

Matthew continued: "We were in the garage, taking inventory of stuff we could use against bad guys, both on and off-planet bad guys, when the shooting started. Rich grabbed the baseball bat, and I grabbed the hose."

"Jon and I waited for Rich and Matt to play whack-a-drone," said Laura. "Then Jon took cellphone pics while I held the yardstick for him."

"Is Alex really an ET?" asked Rita. All attention focused on Rick.

"Yes and no," said Rick with a wink.

• • •

Several NSA agents sat with Rick Henry in his living room. They wore the same black suits. He'd met none of them before. And they all had the last name Jones.

"We haven't been able to identify the manufacturer of the drone that attacked you," said Jones #1.

"Nor have we been able to pinpoint the make of the weapons used," added Jones #2.

Jones #3, their black brother from another mother, just sat there, head buried in his iPad.

"I can understand not being able to identify the drone," said Rick with undisguised sarcasm. "But the machine guns? Come on, guys!"

"Mr. Henry," said Jones #1, "We've had dozens of weapons experts dissecting what was left of that drone. Your son didn't do us any favors with his baseball bat."

"Excuse me, Mr. Henry," said an older man in coveralls who stuck his head into the room.

"Yes, Walter?"

The man held a cellphone, its screen against his chest. "Sir, getting that bullet-proof glass here today is going to cost a pretty penny."

"Walter, I don't care what it costs. I want it installed today."

"Yessir." Walter disappeared as he emphatically relayed Rick's instructions to whomever waited on the other end of the call.

"Now, back to you geniuses," said Rick to the Jones brothers, Moe, Shemp and Cosby. "What *can* you tell me about the machine that almost killed me?"

"Honestly," replied Jones #1, "We are stumped."

Just then, Rick's youngest son burst into the room.

"Jonathan, we're a little busy right now," said Rick.

"Dad, that attacking drone is a Chinese knockoff of the Griff 30, copied from the original one that was manufactured in Norway." Jonathan recited breathlessly. "And those guns were the M249 light Squad Automatic Weapons, or SAW machine guns, made by FN Herstal in Belgium."

"What!" the Jones brothers said in unison.

Jones #3 finally took his head out of his data pad and asked, "Just where might you get this information?"

"Dark Web," said Jonathan, matter-of-factly. "The whole package can be had for the equivalent of $65,000 in Bitcoins. And that includes a thousand rounds of 5.56mm ammo."

"Question," said Rick before any of the Jones doofuses could react. "Do you think we could find out who else bought these in the last few months?"

"I'll bet we could get that answer for another ten grand," said Jonathan.

"Do it!" said Rick, pulling a laminated card out of a secret pocket in his billfold. "Here's my Bitcoin wallet info."

"Roger," said Jonathan as he raced out of the room

"B-b-b-but..." sputtered the gobstruck Jones #3. "...d-d-dat's illegal!"

"This meeting is over," said Rick. "Computer, get my attorney Denver Snuffer on the phone."

• • •

The billionaire next door, as his neighbor had referred to him, found himself tied up in interviews with news media, meetings with his attorney and subsequent ATF representatives moderated by his friend, Federal Judge Clark Waddoups. He flashed his get-out-of-jail-free card to some badly embarrassed NSA minions while accompanied by his buddy the FBI Assistant Special Agent in Charge (ASAC) Bob Lund. Lund previously provided security personnel recommendations for Tabernacle Choir personnel, old chums who retired from the service and wanted to live in Salt Lake City.

During a family meeting behind now quiet, bullet-proof windows, he swore everyone to...well...selective amnesia.

"Did you ever hear from Alex or anyone else in the choir?" asked his wife, Rita.

"Nope. And it's been a month," answered Rick. "Their concert in the Vatican was a grand success. My guess is, they practiced modifying their DNA on the fly until they could all spoof the TSA scanners."

"I saw some streamed clips in the *Church News* online," said Laura. "Richard Elliot even got a standing ovation from the Pope."

"Our limo driver Alex showed up driving one of the tour busses," said Rich.

"Jonathan, you're being quiet," said Rick. "You broke the case wide open."

"Yeah," said his youngest. "But you blew a cool eighty grand on that weaponized drone and *handed it over* to the FBI. Just gave it to them!"

"Yeah, but I also gave the Feebies the shipping address of the Chinese knock-off that attacked us," said Rick.

"And?" asked Rita.

"Let's just say an Idaho group of Satan worshipers is now on the run, with their arsenal of Russian-made ground-to-air missiles and state-of-the-art explosives." Rick smiled as he remembered his conversation with Alex. "These people believe they can thwart the fulfillment of God's return of Enoch City back to Earth, and thereby help the Devil win in the end."

Once again, Matthew wiped the smiles off everyone's faces. "Satan worshipers, huh? Now *these* guys would be interesting people to talk to."

"Matthew David Henry!" scolded his mother.

"No, really Mom," said Matthew. "Especially the tall guy with the tail that we saw on the train. The first words they'll hear after they inevitably and terminally screw up is, 'Hi, I'm the *real* Satan; welcome to Hell.'"

• • •

MAHUJAHPEDIA ENTRY: In the year 7N5793, Mahijah's prophecies were fulfilled when the 160-square-mile city, Mahujah, descended to Earth upon a location called Spring Hill, Missouri, USA. Exhaustive efforts succeeded in evacuating people, livestock, and even animal life from the landing area. A group of self-proclaimed Belial worshipers refused to vacate and are presumed to have gotten their metaphysical questions definitively answered after being crushed.

www.ingramcontent.com/pod-product-compliance
Lightning Source LLC
Chambersburg PA
CBHW050912120626
46552CB00004B/1532